This book belongs to

....

LADYBIRD BOOKS

UK | USA | Canada | Ireland | Australia | India | New Zealand | South Africa

Ladybird Books is part of the Penguin Random House group of companies
whose addresses can be found at global.penguinrandomhouse.com.

www.penguin.co.uk   www.puffin.co.uk   www.ladybird.co.uk

Penguin
Random House
UK

First published 2018
003

Adapted by Lauren Holowaty

Printed in Italy

A CIP catalogue record for this book is available from the British Library

ISBN: 978-0-241-36821-3

All correspondence to:
Ladybird Books
Penguin Random House Children's
80 Strand, London WC2R 0RL

MIX
Paper from
responsible sources
FSC
www.fsc.org   FSC® C018179

Peppa Goes to Scotland

One day, Peppa, George, Mummy and Daddy Pig set off
for Scotland in their camper van.
It was a long journey and Peppa sang all the way:
"We're going to Scotland, we're going to Scotland, in our camper van!"
Soon, the sat nav started singing along as well:
"We're going to Scotland!"
Until finally . . .

"*We have arrived in Scotland*," announced the sat nav.
"Hooray!" cheered Peppa and George.

"Look, Daddy!" said Peppa, pointing to the top of a hill. "There's a castle!"
"Shall we go and see it?" asked Daddy Pig.

"Yes!" said Peppa and George.
They couldn't wait to explore.

"Yes!" said Mummy Pig.
She couldn't wait to get out of the camper van!

At the entrance to the castle, Peppa and her family met Mr McStag.

"Welcome to the best castle in Scotland," he said proudly. "I, Mr McStag, will show you around. But first you must wear these . . ."

Mr McStag held up some kilts.

"I love my kilt!" said Peppa.
"How's yours, Daddy?"

"It's a little draughty,"
said Daddy Pig.

Mr McStag showed them round the castle. He took them to the throne room . . .

. . . and up a secret staircase. "*Oooh-whoo!*" called Peppa, listening for her echo.

"*Oooh-whoo!*" her echo replied.

Then, Mr McStag told them about a mysterious creature that was said to live in the loch nearby. "But no one knows if it is real or a made-up story," he said.
"Mon-sta, ROAR!" yelled George.

"Thank you for showing us the best castle in Scotland!" said Peppa, as they waved goodbye to Mr McStag.
"Mon-sta now?" asked George.
"We'll look for the monster tomorrow, George," said Mummy Pig.
"It's time for bed now."

Luckily, George was just as excited about sleeping in the camper van!

The next morning, Peppa and her family sailed out on to the loch with their guide, Miss Rabbit. "Is the monster real?" asked Peppa. "No one's seen it in all my years working here," said Miss Rabbit.

"Look!" gasped Daddy Pig. "There's the monster."
"That's just a branch, Daddy," said Peppa.
"Oh, yes," said Daddy Pig, a little embarrassed.

Peppa pointed to the
other end of the loch.

"But *that* looks
like the monster!"
she said.

"OK," said Miss Rabbit.
"I'll take us over there.
Hold on tight, everyone!"
Miss Rabbit zoomed the boat
over to the other side of the loch.

But when they got closer, Peppa realized she hadn't seen the monster . . . just some rocks poking out of the water. "Oh," she sighed.

"Is that it over there?" asked Mummy Pig, pointing back to the far side of the loch.

Miss Rabbit turned the boat round and zoomed back the way they'd come.

But when they got there,
all they could see were a
few plants in the water.
"Oh," said Mummy Pig.

Soon Miss Rabbit was zooming the boat round and round in circles all over the loch.

"There it is!
I'm sure of it!"

"No, there it is!"

"It's definitely over there!"

"I think we should head back now," said Miss Rabbit.
"We're all getting a bit dizzy."

Miss Rabbit started to turn the boat round. As she did so,
George, who had been sitting quietly the whole time,
suddenly spotted something behind them . . .

"MON-STA!" called George, as loudly as he could. "MON-STA, ROAR!"

But everyone was too tired
to look round.
"We've stopped looking now,
George," said Mummy Pig.
"I don't think there's a monster
here after all."

All the way back to shore, George had lots of fun talking to the monster, who was following along behind them. No one else noticed a thing.

"ROAR!" said George.

Roar!

Roar!

Roar!

When Miss Rabbit docked the boat, everyone stepped out on to the jetty. George waved goodbye to the monster. "Who are you waving at, George?" asked Mummy Pig.

"Mon-sta friend, mon-sta friend!"
said George, jumping up and down.

Everyone looked over and saw the monster.

"Shiver me timbers!" gasped Miss Rabbit. "I didn't think it existed."

"WOW!" gasped Peppa, Daddy and Mummy Pig.

Just then, the monster dived down into the water and made
a HUGE splash . . .

SPLASH!

Everybody got soaked!

Everyone was very wet, but they were all very happy. Not only had they seen the monster, it had also made them lots of . . .

"Muddy puddles!" cheered Peppa, jumping up and down. Peppa and George love Scotland. Scottish muddy puddles are the best!